Destroyer Escorts

in action

By Al Adcock

Color by Don Greer

Illustrated by Don Greer

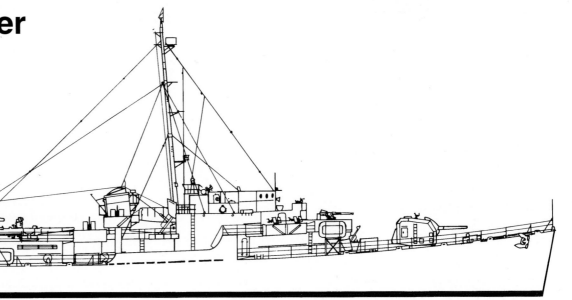

Warships Number 11

squadron/signal publications

The USS HOLDER coming under attack by a Junkers Ju 88 Torpedo planes while escorting a convoy in the Mediterranean off the coast of North Africa on 11 April 1944.

Credits

U.S. Navy
Floating Drydock
Elsilrac Enterprises
Bob Carlisle
Todd Shipyards
Maja Larson
National Archives
Destroyer Escort Sailors Association
U.S. Coast Guard
R.M. Browning Jr
Edmond Anuszczyk
Michel Adam
Mike Slater
Tony Gibbons

ISBN 0-89747-378-7

If you have any photographs of aircraft, armor, soldiers or ships of any nation, particularly wartime snapshots, why not share them with us and help make Squadron/Signal's books all the more interesting and complete in the future. Any photograph sent to us will be copied and the original returned. The donor will be fully credited for any photos used. Please send them to:

Squadron/Signal Publications, Inc.
1115 Crowley Drive
Carrollton, TX 75011-5010

Если у вас есть фотографии самолётов, вооружения, солдат или кораблей любой страны, особенно, снимки времён войны, поделитесь с нами и помогите сделать новые книги издательства Эскадрон/Сигнал ещё интереснее. Мы переснимем ваши фотографии и вернём оригиналы. Имена приславших снимки будут сопровождать все опубликованные фотографии. Пожалуйста, присылайте фотографии по адресу:

Squadron/Signal Publications, Inc.
1115 Crowley Drive
Carrollton, TX 75011-5010

軍用機、装甲車両、兵士、軍艦などの写真を所持しておられる方はいらっしゃいませんか？どの国のものでも結構です。作戦中に撮影されたものが特に良いのです。Squadron/Signal社の出版する刊行物において、このような写真は内容を一層充実し、興味深くすることができます。当方にお送り頂いた写真は、複写の後お返しいたします。出版物中に写真を使用した場合は、必ず提供者のお名前を明記させて頂きます。お写真は下記にご送付ください。

Squadron/Signal Publications, Inc.
1115 Crowley Drive
Carrollton, TX 75011-5010

Ensign Hayden W. Grunder (USNR), pilot of a TBM torpedo bomber, rides the high line from the USS MCCONNELL (DE-163) to the Escort Carrier USS SANGAMON (CVE-26). Ensign Grunder was rescued after his aircraft ran out of gas while on patrol out of Pearl Harbor in February 1945. Destroyer Escorts were called on to perform air-sea rescue, plane guard, convoy escort and sub hunting during World War Two and Korea. (National Archives)

163

Introduction

The concept of the small ocean escort ship began around the turn of the 20th century when there was no real need for such a ship, especially since the United States wasn't at war. However, some fifteen years later there was a real need for an ocean escort ship as German U-boats began roaming the Atlantic like sharks, sinking allied ships during World War One.

The first of the U.S. Navy's escort ships was a small lightly armed torpedo boat that was utilized for coastal defense duties. Constructed at the end of the 19th century, these torpedo boats of the DAHLGREN class were armed with four 4 pound guns and a pair of 18 inch torpedo tubes. They remained in service until around 1910.

During World War One a contract was let by the U.S. Navy for 112 EAGLE boats. The Ford Motor Company won the contract and construction began, however, none were completed by the time the armistice was signed in 1918. These EAGLE boats served between the wars and were used during World War Two in the coastal defense role. One boat, the PE-56, one of eight that served during the war, was lost in 1945 off the coast of New Jersey.

When the United States began supplying the British at the beginning of World War Two, a means to protect convoys crossing the Atlantic was sought. Under the lend-lease program the U.S. provided the British with fifty 4 stack flush deck destroyers to help provide protection for the many convoys. These "flush deckers" were old and not very fast and required constant maintenance to stay serviceable. They did, however, provide a degree of protection until a more adequate solution could be found. The British Admiralty proposed an inexpensive destroyer to escort the convoys. The proposal, designed by Gibbs and Cox, was for a lightly armed and armored ship that could be built in quantity, and very quickly.

The design which became known as the EVARTS class or British Destroyer Escort (BDE) were constructed and commissioned during the 1942-43 time frame. The first fifty were constructed using lend lease funds, although only six went to the British Navy. As soon as the BDEs were commissioned they were put into convoy escort duty in the North Atlantic protecting against U-boat attacks. Once a sufficient number of Destroyer Escorts became available in the Atlantic the number of sinkings by U-boats declined dramatically.

These Destroyer Escorts were also employed along with Escort Carriers (CVEs) in hunter-killer groups that hunted U-boats with surface radar mounted on the DEs and mounted onboard carrier borne Grumman TBF/TBM Avengers. DEs also used the High Frequency/Direction Finding (HF/DF) antenna (known as the *Huff-Duff* antenna) that could locate high frequency radio transmissions from surfaced U-boats. Once located the U-boats were attacked with bombs or depth charges.

Destroyer Escorts were initially armed with three 3inch/50 caliber (76 mm) dual purpose cannons that could be utilized against surface or aerial targets. For anti-aircraft protection two 40mm Bofors cannons and six 20mm Oerlikon cannons were fitted.

For anti-submarine warfare (ASW), depth charge release tracks, roller tracks and throwers were situated around the aft deck and stern area. Two types of depth charges were employed, the MK 6 and MK 8 "Ash Can", and the MK 9 and MK 14 fast sinking types. A Hedgehog 5inch spigot mortar system was placed between the number 1 and 2 3inch gun. The Hedgehog was a throw ahead mortar system that could fire up to 24 mortar rounds in an oval pattern ahead of the ship. They were effective against U-boats up to 300 feet deep.

During World War Two, various camouflage schemes were employed on Destroyer Escorts of the British and American navies. The British used Admiralty camouflage schemes that had

The BARNEY (TB-25), a modified Dahlgren class, was one of the 31 Torpedo Boats built for the U.S. Navy around the turn of the century. Armed with three 3 pound cannons and three torpedo tubes, the BARNEY and her sisters were predecessors to the Ocean Escort design. (ELSILRAC)

The EAGLE BOATS were designed during World War One to be Ocean Escorts for Atlantic convoys. None were completed in time to see service during the war. Following the war they were used in Naval Reserve training roles. EAGLE BOATS were constructed by Ford Motor Company and a few saw service during World War Two. (Floating Drydock)

been developed during World War One and refined during World War Two. The schemes used whites, greys, blues and greens in an attempt to confuse both surface and aerial observers.

The U.S. Navy experimented with various schemes during and after World War One, but since there was no threat to the fleet between the wars, camouflage designs were not top priority and most ships were simply painted gray with large pennant numbers painted on the hull. At the start of World War Two, a need was seen in the North Atlantic for some type of camouflage to confuse observers. The dazzle pattern scheme was initially employed, a scheme that was designed to break up the hull and superstructure outline of the ship. Blacks and various shades of grays were employed, which were effective against surface observers.

As the war continued other schemes were employed that painted the ship a solid color of dark gray or navy blue. This camouflage 'Measure System' was employed when lighting conditions were the best for the ship and the worst for the enemy. The dazzle and solid paint pattern systems were utilized both in the Atlantic and Pacific.

Destroyer Escorts were operated by the U.S. Navy and Britain during World War Two, as well as France and Brazil. Further, the U.S. Coast Guard operated 30 of the EDSALL class Destroyer Escorts, mainly in the Atlantic. The Free French Navy was presented with 6 of the CANNON class for use in the Atlantic, and Brazil operated 8 hunting U-boats.

Following World War Two, those DEs operated by the U.S. Coast guard were returned to U.S. Navy control, while the French and Brazilian Navy retained theirs. When the Korean war broke out in 1950 the U.S. Coast Guard again operated 10 of the same EDSALL class Destroyer Escorts in the Pacific operating as radio and weather ships and also to aid in air-sea rescue along the U.S. to Korea air routes.

The hull of the Destroyer Escort proved to be extremely versatile with conversions to Fast Attack Transports (APD) and Destroyer Escort Radar (DER) ships being undertaken during and following World War Two.

The APD conversions began in 1944 when a need was found for a small fast transport to carry troops to attack remotely held Japanese islands in the pacific. The APDs were also used to transport under water demolition teams (UDT) to Japanese beaches where the "frogmen" would clear underwater obstacles that might impede beach landings. Following the Korean war the U.S. began converting Destroyer Escorts to radar picket ships (DER) used in the "wet" part of the Distant Early Warning (DEW) line in the Atlantic. They served in that capacity into the middle 1960s.

Over 565 Destroyer Escorts and Fast Attack Transports were constructed during and following World War Two, with many more that were slated for construction being canceled. U.S. Destroyer Escorts were named to honor U.S. Navy heroes, former Admirals and Captains as well as former U.S. ships, mainly destroyers. When DEs were converted to APDs, they retained their DE name and only the hull number was changed to reflect their new status. The DEs, DERs and APDs sailored on with many navies of the world some into the 1990's.

The ORANGE (PF-43) was a Frigate built to British RIVER class standards. Frigates had similar armament to the early British Destroyer Escorts (BDE). All of the American Frigates were manned by U.S. Coast Guard crews. Almost 100 Frigates were built during World War Two for coast and convoy patrols. (Floating Drydock)

In a reverse Lend Lease agreement ten British FLOWER class Corvettes were acquired by the U.S. Navy to help to slow the rising tide of German U-boat attacks in the Atlantic during 1942. The SURPRISE (PG-63) ex British HMS HELITROPE is lightly armed with small cannon and is camouflaged in an Admiralty scheme. (Floating Drydock)

One of the first of 50 U.S. Destroyers lent to Britain at the beginning of World War Two was the BUCHANAN (DD-131). As a British destroyer she was named HMS CAMPBELTOWN. The BUCHANAN was launched during World War One and was armed with four 4inch/50 caliber guns. (Floating Drydock)

The PCS-1387 was one of the 58 136 foot wooden hull Sub Chasers completed during World War Two. They were lightly armed with 20mm cannons, Hedgehogs, depth charge throwers and roller racks. The PCSs were slow at 14 knots, but they filled in the gaps hunting subs off the U.S. coast. (Author)

The ROARK (DE-1053) represented a new class of ocean escort ships of the KNOX class. The KNOX class are armed with one 5inch/54 caliber dual purpose cannon, one ASROC (Anti-submarine Rocket) system and one BPDMS (Basic Point Defense Missile System). The KNOX class are capable of 30 knots and displace 4,100 tons, over twice that of the earlier Destroyer Escorts. (Todd Shipyards)

Destroyers and Destroyer Escorts away from their home port were supported by Destroyer Tenders, such as the MARKAB (AD-21, ex AK-31), a former cargo ship. Destroyer Tenders provided a mobile base for heavy maintenance, ammunition and supplies for both DDs and DEs while they were operating on the frontline. (Floating Drydock)

EVARTS CLASS

Following a request by the British government for additional ocean escorts, the EVARTS class was born. Using a Gibbs and Cox marine design that utilized British Admiralty specifications, the first of the British Destroyer Escorts, as they were originally called, were laid down at Mare Island Naval Shipyard in California. The Gibbs and Cox design drew heavily on the success of the British HUNT design. On 22 August 1942, the first of over 500 destroyer escorts slid down the ways, she was the U.S.S. BRENNAN (DE-13). The EVARTS (DE-5) class began with the number designator of DE-5, since the first four of the class went to Britain and were never commissioned as U.S. Ships.

The EVARTS class were 289 feet 5 inches in overall length, this hull length would give the EVARTS class the distinction of being called "short hull." The beam was 35 feet and draught was 10 feet. This shallow draught saved many a destroyer escort from a U-boat torpedo. Standard displacement was rated at 1,150 tons and full war load rating was 1,360 tons. The EVARTS were manned by 15 officers and 180 enlisted grades.

The EVARTS were powered by four General Motors (GM) diesel engines that produced 6,000 horsepower. The diesels drove twin screws through tandem electric motor drives. This combination gave the EVARTS the designation of "GMT" for General Motors Tandem drive. This power plant-drive system gave the EVARTS a flank speed of 20 knots. With 197 tons of available onboard diesel fuel the EVARTS range was 6,000 nautical miles at 12 knots.

Originally the EVARTS were armed with three 3inch/50 caliber MK 21 dual purpose cannons. The 3inch cannon had a muzzle velocity of 2,700 feet per second and a maximum range of 14,600 yards. One quad 1.1 inch anti-aircraft gun mount was situated just forward of the number three 3inch gun. This weapon became the standard intermediate range anti-aircraft weapon until it was replaced by the more effective 40mm Bofors cannon as they became available. The British, however, had replaced the 1.1 mount with the 40mm Bofors weapon early on. Nine 20mm Oerlikon single mount anti-aircraft cannons were placed along the bridge and the upper superstructure. The Oerlikon cannon was a Swiss design built to British and American standards.

EVARTS were further armed with 2 depth charge release tracks at the stern, 8 depth charge throwers amidship, called "K-guns", and the Hedgehog anti-submarine spigot mortar system. Types of depth charges carried were the MK 6 and 8 called "Ash Cans" because of their shape, and the MK 9 and 14 tear drop shaped fast sinking design. The Hedgehog system employed twenty-four 5inch rocket projectiles in a box like container between the number 1 and 2 3inch gun mounts. The 60 pound projectiles had a range of 1,000 feet; the early systems were fixed while the later systems were trainable.

Radar was used for long range air and surface search. Radar, war time nomenclature for "radio detection and ranging", was developed in England and adapted to U.S. ships and aircraft in the late 1930s. For surface search SL radar was employed. The S-band type of radar was placed high up on the main mast in a 42 inch plastic dome. For air search the RCA built SA type of radar was fitted to the main mast. The SA radar was usually referred to as the "bedspring" type of radar because of its resemblance to the bedding item. The Mk 51 gun director was utilized for the 1.1 inch anti-aircraft cannon. The gun director was placed in an open mount pedestal just forward of the 1.1 inch gun.

There were two methods of locating submarines either submerged or on the surface. Underwater detection was handled by QC SONAR. SONAR, an acronym for "sound ranging and navigation", was located in the lower forward hull in a retractable housing. Using echo-location or "pings" a submerged submarine's location could be determined. For surface loca-

The EVARTS (DE-5) was the class leader of the first Destroyer Escorts built for the U.S. Navy. Built by the Boston Navy Yard, she was launched on 7 December 1942. The EVARTS appears to be undergoing a camouflage change from 31/3D as evidenced by the painted out area on the hull. The EVARTS class were armed with three 3inch guns. (Floating Drydock)

tion of a submarine the HF/DF system was employed. Called the "Huff/Duff," a mast mounted antenna would locate surfaced submarine radio signals and home in on them. By using the method of triangulation, the exact location of a radio transmission could be determined

A total of 97 EVARTS class were constructed with 32 of those going to Britain. During the Second World War the British suffered the loss of six of the EVARTS, those being the HMS BLACKWOOD, CAPEL, GOULD, GOODALL, GOODSEN and LAWFORD. The U.S. Navy suffered no loss of this class. Following the Second World War, most of the EVARTS were broken up by 1947 with the exception of WYFFELS (DE-6) and DECKER (DE-47), both of which were given to China in August 1945. The DECKER was sunk in November 1954.

The dazzle camouflage pattern 32/9D shows up quite well on the AUSTIN (DE-15). The AUSTIN was built by Mare Island Navy Yard and launched in 1943. The AUSTIN and all of the EVARTS were 289 feet in length, which were known as "short hulls". (Floating Drydock)

(Below) The FINNEGAN (DE-307) moving at speed off Mare Island Yard, California on 1 September 1944. The FINNEGAN is camouflaged in Measure 32/21D where all vertical surfaces were finished in light gray and dull black. The FINNEGAN, under the command of Lt. Commander H. Huffman sunk an I-Class sub carrying a Kaiten, a Japanese human suicide submarine/torpedo off of Iwo Jima. (Floating Drydock)

(Above) The SMARTT (DE-257) was constructed at Boston Navy Yard and launched in early 1943 just in time for the Battle of the Atlantic. SMARTT is camouflaged in Measure 31/3D, a scheme that employed haze gray, ocean gray and dull black paint. (Navy)

(Below)The BEBAS (DE-10) off of Hunters Point, San Francisco, California during May of 1944. The BEBAS was camouflaged in Measure 32/22D, a pattern that employed light gray and dull black. An HF/DF antenna sits atop the main mast. The HF/DF antenna was used to locate sur-faced submarines by their radio signals. (Navy)

During 1945 the SEDERSTROM (DE-31) is seen moving in close to another ship in preparation for transferring valuable cargo, probably the latest Betty Grable movie. The SEDERSTROM appears to be camouflaged in Measure 17, an ocean gray paint system, although the stack is painted a lighter gray. The area behind the number one 3inch gun is the Hedgehog launcher. (Navy)

The CROWLEY (DE-303) is moored at the outfitting wharf on Mare Island prior to her commissioning in 1944.The CROWLEY is camouflaged in Measure 32/22D. SU and SA radar are atop the main mast. The radio direction finder is located above the bridge. (Navy)

Armament Development

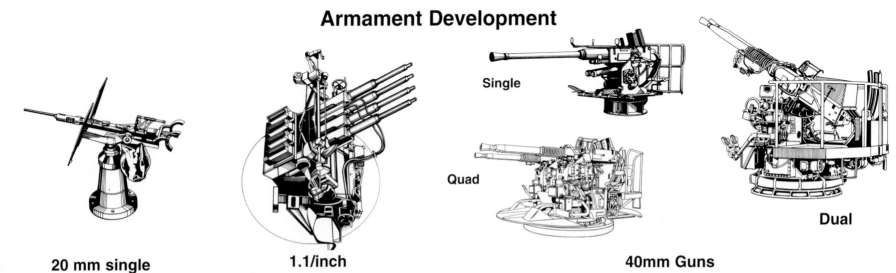

20 mm single

1.1/inch

Single

Quad

40mm Guns

Dual

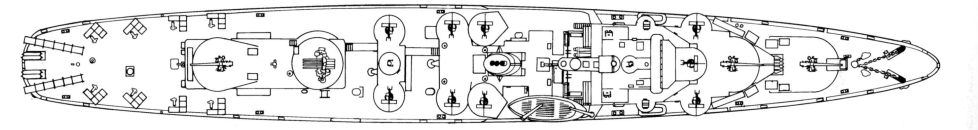

DE 303 USS Crowley

Length:	289' 5"
Beam:	35'
Draft:	10'
Displacement	
Standard:	1150 tons
...Full Load:	1360
Propulsion:	6,000 HP Diesel Electric
Speed:	20 Knots
Complement:	200
Armament:	3 x 3"/50 guns
	1 x 1.1" Quad AA
	8 x 20mm AA
	Depth Charges

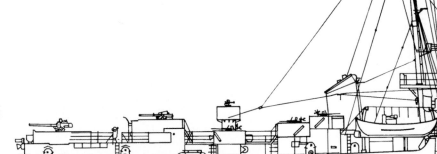

BUCKLEY CLASS

The BUCKLEY class introduced changes from the earlier EVARTS class that would be incorporated in all subsequent classes. The first of the changes was the hull being lengthened to 306 feet, and the second was the addition of triple torpedo tubes.

The 306 foot hull length was dictated by the steam power plant. Two Foster-Wheeler boilers provided the steam for the General Electric turbo-electric geared turbines which drove the twin screws. The turbo-electric drive gave the BUCKLEY class the designator of "TE." The available 12,000 shaft horsepower gave the BUCKLEY class a design rated speed of 23.5 knots. The 306 foot hull length of the BUCKLEYs were referred to as "long hulls," in contrast to the "short hulled" Evarts. The BUCKLEYs had a beam of 36 feet 10 inches and a draught of 14 feet. Displacement was 1,400 tons standard and 1,720 tons full war load. With 340 tons of fuel onboard, a range of 5,000 miles at 12 knots was possible. Complement was 15 officers and 198 enlisted men.

The BUCKLEY class was originally armed with three 3inch/50 caliber dual purpose open mount cannons, a single 1.1 inch quad anti-aircraft open mount, and six 20mm cannons completed the armament suite. A triple torpedo tube launcher was mounted amidship on the superstructure. Mark 15 torpedoes were carried in the launcher. No torpedo tubes were carried by the British lend-lease CAPTAIN class Destroyer Escorts, nor was the quad 1.1 inch mount, that weapon being replaced by a single or twin 40mm. For anti-submarine duties depth charge throwers, roller racks and the hedgehog system were fitted. As the war wore on improvements were made to the armament. The 1.1 inch weapon was replaced by a twin 40mm Bofors mount., and to increase anti-aircraft protection, the triple torpedo launcher was removed and 4 single "army type" 40mm cannons were placed in their stead. On eleven ships the 3inch weapons were replaced by two 5inch/38 caliber dual purpose cannons in an enclosed mount.

Originally over 100 3inch to 5inch conversions were authorized, but only eleven were completed. Eventually twelve 20mm cannons were fitted to increase close in anti-aircraft protection.

Radar, sonar and HF/DF antennas remained the same as in the EVARTS, although a few of the BUCKLEYS were fitted with SS surface search radar. When the 5inch mounts replaced the 3inch ones, the two Mk 52 radar controlled gun directors replaced the single Mk 51 director.

Fifty of the BUCKLEY class were selected for conversion to fast attack transport (APD), but by the time the war ended less than 46 had actually been converted. A total of 154 of the BUCKLEY class were constructed by eight different ship yards on the Atlantic and Pacific coasts, inland at Pittsburgh, Pennsylvania, and on the Gulf of Mexico making them the most widely built of the Destroyer Escorts. Forty-six of the BUCKLEYS went to Britain under the lend-lease program and were placed in the CAPTAIN class. Both the British and the U.S. Navy lost two BUCKLEYS during World War Two. The HMS BICKERTON (ex DE-75) and the BULLEN (ex DE-78) were lost to U-boat attacks. A further eight were so severely damaged by mines or torpedoes that they were not repaired or returned to the US. The UNDERHILL (DE-682) was sunk by a Japanese midget submarine on 24 July 1945 off the Philippines and the RICH (DE-695) was lost on 8 June 1944 during the allied Normandy invasion. The DONNELL (DE-56) was severely damaged by a torpedo on 3 May 1944 while on convoy duty in the Atlantic. The ship was saved and she was used first to supply electricity at Cherbourg, France and then she was towed to England and used as a barracks ship. As a barracks ship she was classified as the 1X-182.

Following World War Two the U.S. Navy gave many of the BUCKLEYS to Taiwan, South Korea, Mexico, Chile and other countries. The balance were placed in service with U.S. Naval reserve forces.

The FOGG (DE-57) being outfitted at Bethlehem Hingham Shipyard, Mass., sits alongside the HMS BENTINCK (EX USS BULL DE-52) in July 1943. The FOGG wears camouflage Measure 22, while the BENTINCK is finished in Admiralty colors. The railing mounted on the front of the 3inch gun tubs prevent the guns from being lowered and firing into the hull. (Navy)

The BUCKLEY (DE-51), was the lead ship in the new class of "long hull" Destroyer Escorts built for the U.S. Navy with a hull length of 300 feet at the waterline. The BUCKLEY is camouflaged in Measure 22, utilizing haze gray and navy blue. (Floating Drydock)

EICHENBERGER (DE-202) leaving Charleston Navy Yard in November 1943, wearing camouflage Measure 13, the haze gray system. The 1.1 inch gun position is covered to conceal the presence of the weapon. SL and SA radar are fitted to the main mast. (Navy)

The SCOTT (DE-214) carries a triple torpedo tube amidship between the stack and the Mk 51 gun director. The Mk 51 director was utilized by the 1.1 and 40mm anti-aircraft guns. The SCOTT was named to commemorate Rear Admiral Norman Scott who was killed during the battle off Guadalcanal in November 1942. The SCOTT was later converted to a High Speed Transport (APD). (Navy)

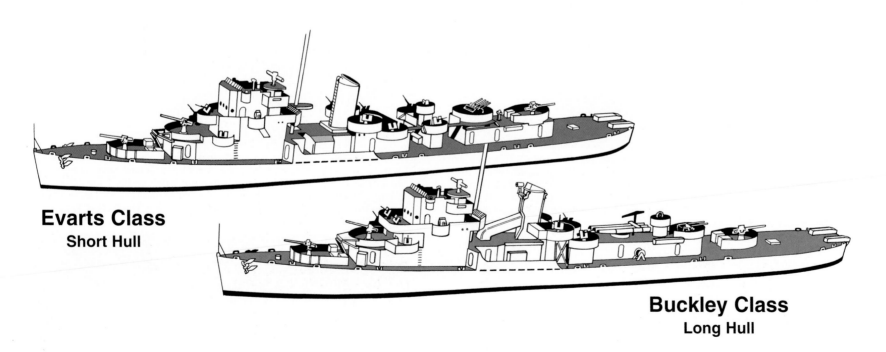

Evarts Class
Short Hull

Buckley Class
Long Hull

(Below) REUBEN JAMES (DE-153) in the Atlantic on a trials cruise prior to her commissioning in April 1943. No depth charges are fitted to the roller racks or the "K" guns. The ship is riding high, the black boot topping is showing on the Measure 22 paint scheme. The REUBEN JAMES was converted to a radar picket ship (DER) in 1945. (Navy)

(Above) The SOLAR (DE-221), riding very high in the water, moves alongside an oiler in April 1944. The torpedo tubes have been replaced by 20mm and 40mm anti-aircraft guns. The aft mast contains the HF/DF antenna. The SOLAR is camouflaged in Measure 22. The SOLAR was destroyed by an internal explosion on 30 April 1946. (Navy)

(Below) A service yard craft re-supplies the BURKE (DE-215) in June 1944. The torpedo tubes have been replaced by four single 40mm guns, although the 1.1 inch gun is still in place. The BURKE was converted to APD 65 in 1945 and in 1968 she was sold to Columbia. The BURKE is painted in Measure 22.

(Below) The HARMON (DE-678) now mounts new enclosed 5inch/38 guns. The bridge contours were also changed and the Hedgehogs are closer to the bridge. The HARMON was one of 11 BUCKLEY class to be so converted. The HARMON was camouflaged in Measure 22 paint scheme. (Navy)

(Above) The ENGLAND (DE-635) was one of the most highly decorated Destroyer Escorts. She was credited with sinking six Japanese RO subs in twelve days in May-June 1944. The Japanese got their revenge one year later when a Kamikaze attack severely damaged her off of Okinawa. (Navy)

(Below) An ice covered SPANGLER (DE-696) sits wharf side. The SPANGLER was constructed by Defoe at Bay City Michigan and launched in July 1943. SPANGLER is camouflaged in Measure 17. (Navy)

(Below) The WEEDEN (DE-797) carrying a modified anti-air-craft suite of four 40mm guns in single mounts which required removal of the triple torpedo tubes. Two 20mm cannons were added between the depth charge roller racks and the number three 3inch gun mount. The WEEDEN is camouflaged in Measure 22. The additional aft mounted mast contains the HF/DF antenna. (Navy)

(Above) The CURRIER (DE-700) is camouflaged in an open Measure 31-32/14D which consisted of dull black and ocean-haze, colors which could be loosely interpreted by the painter. Technicians appear to be working on the range find-er. The CURRIER was constructed by Defoe, Bay City, Michigan. (Navy)

(Below) HOLLIS (DE-794) is finished in the open Measure 31-32/14D. Compare this application to that of the CURRI-ER (DE-700). The HOLLIS was constructed by Consolidated, Orange, Texas and launched on 11 September 1943. (Navy)

(Below) The SPANGENBERG (DE-223) during builder's trials in the Atlantic in 1943. The mast contains an HF/DF antenna as well as an SL radar antenna in a covered dome. She is finished in Measure 22. (Navy)

(Above) The THOMASON (DE-203) is camouflaged in Measure 31/16D, a scheme drawn for the ALLEN SUMNER (DD-692) class, as well as the BUCKLEY class, and the BALTIMORE class cruisers, and CALIFORNIA class battleships. The design was of course modified to fit each class of ship. The THOMASON was constructed by Charleston Navy Yard and launched on 23 August 1943. (Navy)

(Below) HMS HALSTED (K-556), formerly REYNOLDS (DE-91), was loaned to Britain under lend lease and placed in the CAPTAIN Class (Second Group). British DE's were not equipped with torpedo tubes, opting instead for more anti-aircraft guns. She was severely damaged by a German E-Boat and not repaired. The HALSTED is camouflaged in an Admiralty disruptive pattern. (National Archives)

17

CANNON CLASS

The CANNON class retained the long hull of the BUCKLEY class, but reverted back to diesel power, thus they were designated as "DET" for diesel-electric tandem motor drive.

The CANNON class was powered by four General Motors Corporation diesel engines producing 1,500 horsepower each for a total of 6,000 horsepower (6,000 horsepower less than the BUCKLEY class). The diesel engines that powered twin screws through tandem electric motor drives were the same type of diesels used in U.S. Navy submarines. Speed was rated at 21 knots, but in reality the ships strained to do 18 knots. With 315 tons of onboard fuel, range was rated at 10,000 nautical miles.

The hull was 306 feet overall and 300 feet at the waterline. Beam was 36 feet 10 inches and draught was rated at 14 feet. Displacement was 1,240 tons standard and 1,520 tons full war load. The CANNON class retained a bridge structure similar to the BUCKLEY class, as well as a similar armament suite.

The CANNON class was originally armed with three 3inch/50 caliber open mount dual purpose cannons, twin 40mm anti-aircraft Bofors cannons and up to eight 20mm cannons. A triple torpedo launcher was located on the mid-ship superstructure. Later in the war the torpedo launcher was removed and four 40mm single mounts were installed in its place. This change was made for two reasons. The U.S. Navy found that the DE's were not utilizing the torpedo launcher to carry out surface attacks with torpedoes, and additional anti-aircraft protection was needed.

For anti-submarine duties a pair of depth charge release tracks were placed on the stern. Eight roller racks and eight Mk 6 depth charge "K" gun projectors were placed four per side. Mk 6 and Mk 8 Ash Cans and Mk 9 and 11 fast sinking depth charges were employed. A Hedgehog spigot mortar system was placed between the number one and two 3inch gun mounts. Between the depth charge release tracks were a pair of smoke generators. The smoke generators could be used to produce smoke to hide other ships in a convoy or an assembled fleet.

The CANNON class originally was equipped with SL surface search radar with a range of 12 miles, but that was replaced by the improved SU radar with a range of 20 miles. For air search an SA, "bedspring" antenna was placed at the top of the mast. QC sonar was located on the lower forward hull in a retractable housing.

A Huff/Duff (HF/DF) antenna was placed either on the main mast or on an auxiliary mast on the aft superstructure. The HF/DF antenna was used to locate surfaced submarines broadcasting in the high frequency band.

One of the CANNON class was involved in the top secret RAINBOW PROJECT, commonly referred to as the PHILADELPHIA EXPERIMENT. The project, which began in June 1943 at the Philadelphia Navy Yard, utilized the ELDRIDGE (DE-173) as a test ship. Two high capacity 75 kVA generators were reportedly placed on the deck and they supplied electric power to magnetic coils. The idea was to make the ELDRIDGE disappear by electronic camouflage. Supposedly, in one test the ELDRIDGE disappeared from Philadelphia and instantly reappeared off of Norfolk, Virginia. Following the "experiment" the ELDRIDGE was reconfigured back to her original fighting condition and she returned to convoy duty in the Atlantic.

A total of 72 of the CANNON class were constructed by Dravo and Federal on the Atlantic, Western Pipe and Steel on the Pacific and Tampa Shipbuilding on the Gulf of Mexico. Eight went to Brazil (DE-99-101, 174-175 and 177-179), including the class leader CANNON (DE-99) which became the Brazilian BAEPENDI. The French took possession of six of the CANNON class (DE-106-111). They joined the Free French 5th Destroyer Division in 1944. The

The CANNON (DE-99) was launched in 1943 and was the class leader. The CANNON class became known as the DET for diesel-electric tandem drive. The CANNON was loaned to Brazil in December 1944 and renamed the BAEPENDI. Eventually eight of the CANNON class would be loaned to Brazil. The CANNON is finished in Measure 22. (ELSILRAC)

French specified no torpedo tubes and increased 40mm anti-aircraft protection.

Following World War Two, 49 of the CANNON class were presented to China, Holland, France, Uruguay, Japan, Philippines, Greece, Italy, Peru, Thailand, and South Korea under the International Logistics Program (ILP).

The SLATER (DE-766), which had been presented to the Greek Navy in March of 1951, was purchased by a group of U.S. investors and towed back to the United States in 1992 after serving Greece for 41 years. The SLATER was refurbished and is now on display in New York City alongside the U.S. aircraft carrier INTREPID (CV-11).

The BREEMAN (DE-104) leaving Norfolk Navy Yard on 10 February 1944. The Huff-Duff (HF/DF) antenna is high atop the main mast. The Measure 22 scheme was the finish preferred in the central Atlantic area of operations. The BREEMAN was given to China in 1948. (Navy)

The THORNHILL (DE-195) escorting a pair of tankers out of safe harbor in July 1944. The THORNHILL is camouflaged in Measure 31/3D. The THORNHILL'S torpedo tubes have been removed in favor of increased 40mm anti-aircraft protection. Long range wire antennas and HF/DF antenna have been installed on the upper superstructure. (Navy)

The ACREE (DE-167) lies at anchor off Hunters Point, San Francisco, California in February 1945. The ACREE is camouflaged in Measure 21, the navy blue system. The ACREE served in the U.S. Navy until 1972 when she was stricken from the rolls. (Navy)

The ELDRIDGE (DE-173) entering harbor in September 1943. In June of 1943 The ELDRIDGE was involved with the infamous PHILADELPHIA EXPERIMENT, also known as PROJECT RAINBOW. For 50 years the secret, if any exists, has been kept. The ELDRIDGE, as seen here is finished in Measure 31/3D, a design originally drawn for the EVARTS class. In 1951 the ELDRIDGE was turned over to Greece. (Navy)

Depth Charges and Roller Tracks

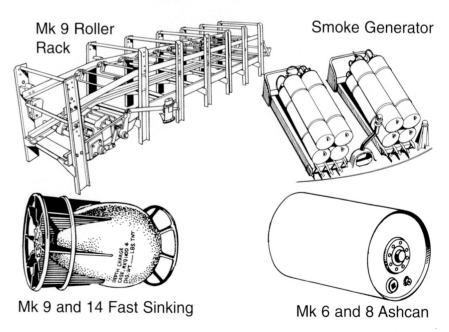

Mk 9 Roller Rack

Smoke Generator

Mk 9 and 14 Fast Sinking

Mk 6 and 8 Ashcan

(Below) CLARENCE L. EVANS (DE-113) leaving the Philadelphia Navy Yard on 7 July 1944. She is finished in open Measure 31-32/14D. The triple torpedo tubes have been removed for the addition of single Bofors 40mm AA guns. She was loaned to France in 1952. (Navy)

(Above) The RIDDLE (DE-185) transferring official mail to the ELDORA-DO (AGC-11), an Amphibious Forces Flagship, in February 1945, just prior to the invasion of Iwo Jima. The RIDDLE was part of the escort for the invasion force. The RIDDLE is camouflaged in Measure 21, although the stack appears to be in a lighter shade of gray. (Navy)

(Below)The STRAUB (DE-181) in 1944 is camouflaged in Measure 31/3D. She was built by Federal and launched in 1943. The aft mast contains the HF/DF antenna used to locate surfaced submarines broadcasting in the high frequency band. (Navy)

(Below) The McANN (DE-179) just before being turned over to Brazil in 1944 where she was renamed the BRACUI. The McANN is camouflaged in Measure 22, the Graded System. The BRACUI remained in Brazilian service until she was scrapped in 1974. (Navy)

(Above) The FNV SENEGALAIS T-22 (formerly DE 106) serving with the French 5th Destroyer Division in 1945. The SENEGALAIS is camouflaged in Measure 22, the Graded System. All French CANNON Class DEs had their triple torpedo tubes removed in favor of 40mm anti-aircraft guns. The aft mast contains the HF/DF antenna and the main mast is fitted with SL and SA radar. (Via Michel Adam)

(Below)The FNV TUNISIEN (T-23) was the ex CROSLEY (DE-108) that was given to the Free French Naval Forces in 1944. The main mast contains the HF/DF antenna and the SL radar. Note the different antenna arrangement on the SENEGALAIS. The TUNISIEN was returned to the U.S. in 1964 and scrapped. (Navy)

21

(Below) The TILLS (DE-748) moving at high speed during 1944. The TILLS is camouflaged in an open Measure 31-32/10D. The upper main mast is fitted with the SA radar antenna and the SU radar is mounted on a mast extension. The TILLS served with the U.S. Navy until 1964 when she was expended as a target. (Navy)

(Above) The PARKS (DE-165) during her builder's shakedown cruise in July 1943. The PARKS is camouflaged in Measure 22. The main mast is fitted with SA and SL radar antennas. CANNON class DEs were fitted with three 3inch dual purpose cannons. (Navy)

(Below) The OSTERHAUS (DE-164) in the Atlantic out from Newark, New Jersey in June 1943 during sea trials. SA and SL radar antennas are on the main mast. Once the OSTERHAUS enters fleet service the DE designator on the hull will be removed. The OSTERHAUS is camouflaged in Measure 22. (Floating Drydock)

(Below)The TRUMPETER (DE-180) on sea trials in October 1943. The Weapons Officer is conducting a test of the triple torpedo launcher. The HF/DF antenna is placed high upon the main mast with the SL antenna placed just below it. The TRUMPETER is camouflaged in Measure 22, the standard finish for the Atlantic in 1943. (Floating Drydock)

(Above)The CATES (DE-763), during builder's trials in Tampa Bay in 1943. The CATES has the new 20mm and 40mm gun limiters in place on the midship guns. The CATES is fitted with HF/DF, SL and SA antennas, as well as the new MK-52 gun director. (Navy)

(Below) The EISNER (DE-192) moving out of New York Navy Yard in July 1944. The EISNER is camouflaged in Measure 31/3D modified for the CANNON class. The main mast is fitted with SL and SA radar, while the aft mast has an HF/DF antenna fitted. The EISNER was sent to Holland in May 1951. (Navy)

23

(Above) The BARON (DE-166) leaving Mare Island Navy Yard in 1944. The BARON is camouflaged in Measure 31/3D a scheme that was originally drawn for the EVARTS class. The BARON was sent to Uruguay in May of 1952 and renamed the URUGUAY (UNV-1) where she served until 1990. (Floating Drydock)

The KYNE (DE-744) made a port call to St. Petersburg, Florida in 1956 while serving with the Atlantic Naval Reserve Training Fleet. The KYLE carries Measure 27, the blue/gray scheme. All of the 20mm guns have been removed. The KYNE served as a Naval Reserve Training Ship until 1972 when she was scrapped. (Author)

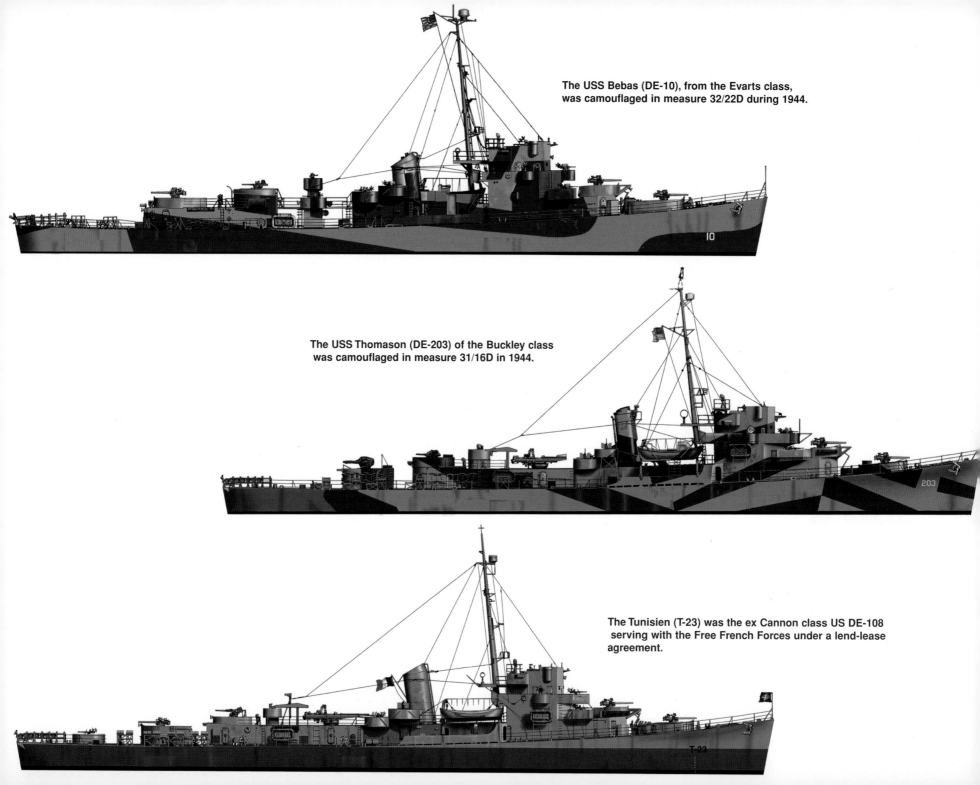

The USS Bebas (DE-10), from the Evarts class, was camouflaged in measure 32/22D during 1944.

The USS Thomason (DE-203) of the Buckley class was camouflaged in measure 31/16D in 1944.

The Tunisien (T-23) was the ex Cannon class US DE-108 serving with the Free French Forces under a lend-lease agreement.

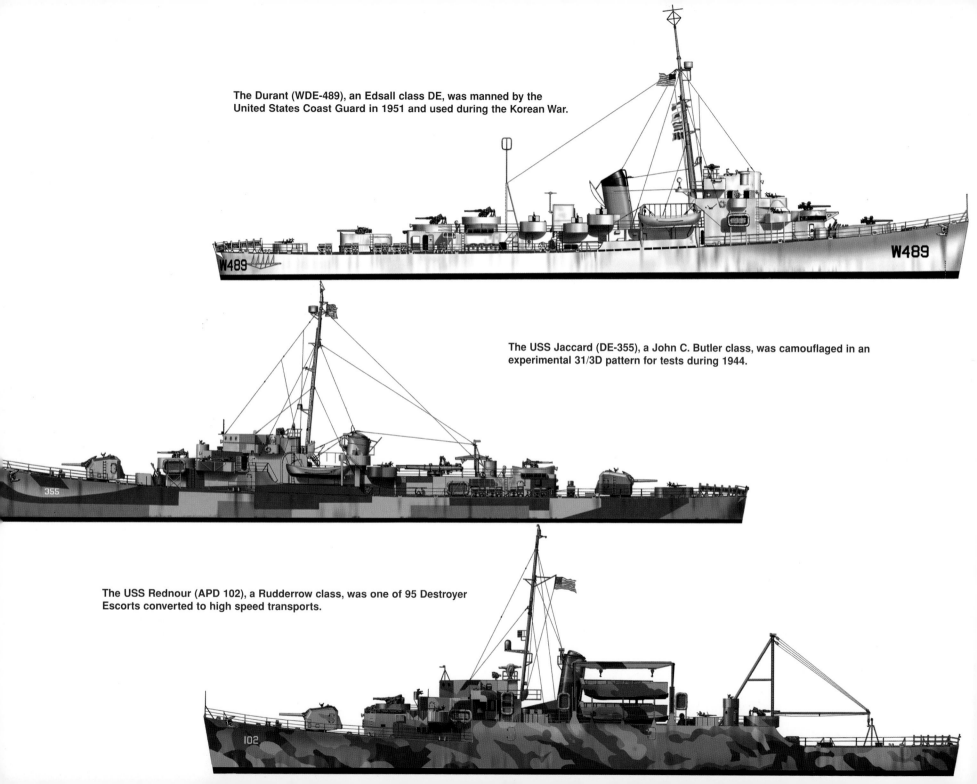

The Durant (WDE-489), an Edsall class DE, was manned by the
United States Coast Guard in 1951 and used during the Korean War.

The USS Jaccard (DE-355), a John C. Butler class, was camouflaged in an
experimental 31/3D pattern for tests during 1944.

The USS Rednour (APD 102), a Rudderrow class, was one of 95 Destroyer
Escorts converted to high speed transports.

EDSALL CLASS

The EDSALL class retained the standard long hull design of the two earlier classes, but a new engine-gear drive combination was introduced. The power plant selected for the EDSALL class was the Fairbanks-Morse 38D8-1/8-10 diesel engine that produced 1,500 horsepower each; the four installed diesels produced a total of 6,000 horsepower. The diesels drove twin screws through a reverse gear drive giving the EDSALLS a rated speed of 21 knots. With the available 315 tons of fuel a range of 11,000 nautical miles was possible at 12 knots.

The EDSALL class was 306 feet in overall length and 300 feet at the waterline. Beam was 36 feet 10 inches and draught was 11 feet. Displacement was 1,200 tons standard and 1,490 tons full war load. Complement was 15 officers and 201 enlisted men. The EDSALL Class was constructed by two builders, Brown Shipbuilding of Houston and Consolidated Steel of Orange, both in Texas on the coast of the Gulf of Mexico.

The EDSALL class was armed with three 3inch/50 caliber dual purpose open mount cannons, a twin 40mm Bofors open mount anti-aircraft cannon and eight 20mm close in anti-aircraft cannons. A triple 21 inch torpedo launcher was installed on the superstructure amidship. Eventually the torpedo launcher was removed in favor of increased anti-aircraft protection in the form of 4 single mount 40mm Bofors "army type" cannons. The 20mm cannon mounts were also increased with the installation of an open tub containing a pair of weapons between the depth charge release tracks. For anti-submarine duties a pair of depth charge release tracks were placed at the stern. Further, 8 roller racks and 8 "k" gun depth charge projectors were placed just forward of the release tracks. The hedgehog mortar system was in between the number 1 and 2 3inch gun positions. Following a collision in 1945 the CAMP (DE-251) had her 3inch cannons replaced with a pair of 5inch/38 caliber cannons in enclosed mounts.

The EDSALL class was equipped with SL surface search radar, however, this system was replaced with the improved SU radar as the sets became available. For air search the SA radar was employed using the distinctive antenna known as the "bedspring". The sonar suite consisted of the QC type that was housed in a retractable dome at the forward lower hull area. For submarine hunting, a Huff/Duff (HF/DF) antenna was fitted which located submarines operating their radios in the high frequency band.

A total of 85 EDSALL class DEs were constructed and of those 30 were operated by U.S. Coast Guard (USCG) crews mainly on convoy duty in the North Atlantic and Mediterranean. It was on one of these convoy routes that the LEOPOLD (DE-319) was torpedoed (10 March 1944 by a German Acoustic Torpedo). The LEOPOLD was the only Destroyer Escort lost by a USCG crew during World War Two. The next three losses were U.S. Navy operated. On 11 April 1944 the HOLDER (DE-401) was attacked with torpedoes in the Mediterranean off the coast of North Africa by Luftwaffe Ju-88s. The HOLDER took a hit on the port side and was mortally wounded. She was taken under tow to New York where it was discovered that the damage was too severe to be repaired and she was broken up for parts. The stern was "donated" to the torpedoed MENGES (DE-320), a USCG operated Destroyer Escort. The balance of the HOLDER was converted to a moored training ship (MTS) and used to train destroyer escort crews. A 5inch enclosed gun was installed in place of the 3inch mount. German torpedoes in the Atlantic also took out the FREDERICK C. DAVIS (DE-136) and the FISKE (DE-143).

Following World War Two, all of the USCG manned Destroyer Escorts were returned to U.S. Navy control. This change of ownership didn't last long; when the Korean War broke out in 1950 the USCG again needed ocean escorts for the Pacific Convoy route from the U.S. to Korea. Twelve of the former EDSALL USCG manned DEs were commissioned as USCG

The EDSALL (DE-129), class leader, in 1944 after the removal of the triple torpedo tubes and installation of the 20mm and 40mm guns in their place. EDSALL class DEs were powered by four Fairbanks-Morse diesel engines with reverse angle drive. Thus, the class became known as the FMR. The modification also included the installation of 20mm gun tubs between the number 3 3inch gun and the depth charge roller racks. The EDSALL is camouflaged in an open measure 31-32/3D. (US Navy)

ships and converted to USCG standards. Six of the EDSALLS were configured as radio/weather ships with a weather balloon shelter placed on the superstructure just aft the stack. Following the Korean War USCG operated DEs were returned to U.S. Navy control.

34 of the EDSALL class were converted to Destroyer Escort, Radar (DER) standards during the 1950's and used in the "wet" DEW line in the Atlantic Ocean.

An example of the EDSALL class, the STEWART (DE-238) is preserved as a memorial at Galveston, Texas on Galveston Bay not far from where she was launched from Brown Shipbuilding in 1943.

The crew of the CHATELAIN (DE-149) prepares the ship for sea duty on 8 May 1944. Less than one month later the CHATELAIN and her sister ship PILLSBURY (DE-133) along with GUADALCANAL (CVE-60) would capture the German submarine U-505. For their action all three ships were awarded the Presidential Unit Citation. The CHATELAIN, call sign "FRENCHY", was camouflaged in Measure 22 for service in the Atlantic. (Floating Drydock)

The NEUNZER (DE-150) under way in the Atlantic during 1944. The black boot topping shows just below the measure 22 paint scheme. The torpedo loading hatch is in the open position just below the torpedo loading crane. The NEUNZER has additional 20mm guns on the fantail between the number 3 gun position and the roller tracks. (Floating Drydock)

The OTTERSTETTER (DE-244) rides at anchor prior to a sortie in the Atlantic during the summer of 1944. The aft/auxiliary mast contains the HF/DF antenna used to locate U-boats broadcasting in the high frequency band. The main mast is fitted with SL radar. The OTTERSTETTER is camouflaged in Measure 22 scheme. (Floating Drydock)

Radar and Radio Antenna

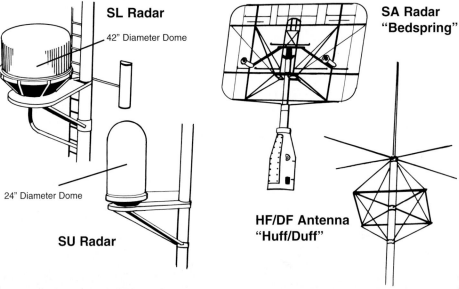

SL Radar

42" Diameter Dome

SA Radar "Bedspring"

24" Diameter Dome

SU Radar

HF/DF Antenna "Huff/Duff"

(Below) The VANCE (DE-387) was one of 30 DEs manned by US Coast Guard crews during World War Two. VANCE is camouflaged in Measure 31/3D. The HF/DF antenna is on the auxiliary aft mast, and the SL and SA radar screen are fitted to the main mast. The VANCE also served under a Coast Guard crew during the Korean Conflict. Eventually the VANCE would be converted to a DER. (U.S. Coast Guard)

(Above)The BRISTER (DE-327) sails out of the Norfolk Navy Yard in 1944 for service in the Atlantic. The BRISTER is camouflaged in Measure 31/3D. The main mast is fitted with SL surface search and the "Bedspring" SA air search antenna. (Navy)

(Below) Following her torpedoing by a Luftwaffe Ju-88 in the Mediterranean Sea, HOLDER (DE-401) was towed to the U.S. Her stern was "donated" to the damaged MENGES (DE-320). The remainder of the ship was repaired enough that she could be utilized as a moored training ship (MTS). A 5inch enclosed gun replaced the number one 3inch weapon. (ELSILRAC)

Torpedo Launcher and 21 inch Torpedo

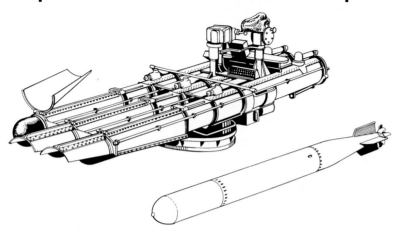

21 inch Mk 15 Torpedo

(Below)The watch mans the bridge as the INCH (DE-146) moves at speed in the Atlantic in late 1943. The INCH is in the then standard Measure 22 scheme. The gun limiters for the 20mm guns can be seen on the bridge and superstructure mounts. (Navy)

(Above) A bow to stern view of the triple torpedo tubes on the JACOB JONES (DE-130). This Destroyer Escort was named for the earlier "Flush Deck" Destroyer JACOB JONES (DD-130) that was sunk in the Atlantic by the German U-578, a Type VIIC U-boat. (Floating Drydock)

The MENGES (DE-320) in the Atlantic, manned by a USCG crew, was damaged by a German torpedo and was repaired by using the stern from the severely damaged HOLDER. Bottom to top are seen the 20mm mounts, triple torpedo tubes, twin 40mm, depth charge roller racks, 3inch gun, more 20mm guns in tubs, and the depth charge roller tracks. The item between the life rafts is the MK-51 gun director. (Navy)

The CHAMBERS (DE-391) undergoes a change of ownership from the U.S. Navy to the U.S. Coast Guard on 11 June 1952. As a USCG ship she was renumbered as the WDE-491 to avoid confusion with U.S. Navy numbering. The CHAMBERS was used during the Korean Conflict along the air/sea convoy route in the Pacific. (U.S. Coast Guard)

The DURANT (WDE-489) in USCG service during 1952. In U.S. Navy service she was designated DE-389, and was used during the Korean Conflict as a weather and radio ship along the U.S. to Korea air/sea convoy route. In USCG service the DURANT is painted overall white, the standard "peace time" scheme. (U.S. Coast Guard)

RUDDEROW CLASS

The RUDDEROW class retained the long hull of the earlier classes, but returned to steam as its motive power. Also introduced was a new bridge design that closely resembled the style of the ALLEN M. SUMNER class Destroyers. Armament was upgraded to 5inch guns which gave the RUDDEROW class the designator of "TEV" (TE for turbo electric drive, V for 5inch guns.

The RUDDEROW class had a hull length of 306 feet overall and 300 feet at the waterline. Beam was 36 feet 10 inches and draught was rated at 11 feet 2 inches with full load. Displacement was 1,430 tons standard and 1,811 tons full war loaded. Power for the twin screws was provided by 12,000 horsepower Babcock and Wilcox boilers that produced steam for the twin General Electric turbo electric geared turbines. On trials the RUDDEROW class managed 24 knots, more than adequate to be able to keep up with convoys and escort carriers (CVEs). With 324 tons of onboard fuel oil a range of 6,000 miles was possible at a cruising speed of 13 knots.

The RUDDEROW class introduced the use of the 5inch/38 caliber dual purpose naval cannon. The 5inch gun could be used against both surface and anti-aircraft targets. The 5inch gun

had a muzzle velocity of 2,600 feet per second and a range of 37,000 feet against aerial targets. Two of the 5inch enclosed mounts replaced the three 3inch/50 caliber open mounts. The 5inch gun was able to fire the new proximity fuse round that greatly increased the anti-aircraft effectiveness of the RUDDEROW class. A pair of twin 40mm Bofors cannons were installed, one fore and one aft. Twelve 20mm cannons were fitted, 10 on the superstructure and 2 just forward of the depth charge release tracks. 8 roller racks and 8 "K" gun projectors were placed along side of the aft deck sides. A Hedgehog system was placed between the forward 5inch gun and the 40mm twin cannons.

A triple 21 inch torpedo launcher was fitted to the superstructure just aft of the stack. The launcher was eventually removed in favor of 4 single mount 40mm Bofors for increased anti-aircraft protection. A few of the RUDDEROW class had the aft twin 40mm mount replaced by a quad 40mm beginning in 1945.

A total of 62 of the RUDDEROW class were constructed by six different shipyards, but only 22 were completed and commissioned as Destroyer Escorts, the balance were completed as Fast Attack Transports (APD). Following World War Two all of the RUDDEROW class were placed in naval reserve forces and used for training.

The HOLT (DE-706) was presented to Korea on 13 June 1968 and the RILEY (DE-579) went to Taiwan as the TAI YUAN.

The RUDDEROW (DE-224), was the class leader of 72 ships. Completed in 1944 the RUDDEROW was armed with two 5inch dual purpose guns in enclosed mounts, and two twin mounted 40mm anti-aircraft cannons, and ten 20mm guns. The RUDDEROW is camouflaged in Measure 22, a scheme employed both in the Atlantic and Pacific Theaters. (Floating Drydock)

The main 5inch gun and the aft 40mm guns of the DAY (DE-225) train on the photographing aircraft in 1944. The main mast is fitted with SA and SL radar antennas, while the aft mast contains the sub-hunting HF/DF antenna. The DAY is camouflaged in Measure 22. (Floating Drydock)

A starboard side view of the HODGES (DE-231) shows the Measure 32,33/3D open Measure camouflage scheme as she sails past a net ship (AN). The main mast is fitted with the new SU antenna, surface search radar, and the SA "bedspring" air search radar. The low silhouette of the wheel house and bridge are evident. (Floating Drydock)

The CHAFFEE (DE-230) sails into harbor in 1944. The CHAFFEE is camouflaged in Measure 22, the graded system that utilized navy blue and haze gray paint that was designed to make the ship appear farther away than she actually was. The ready round canister for the Hedgehogs can be seen below the forward 40mm mount. (Floating Drydock)

Main Armament Development

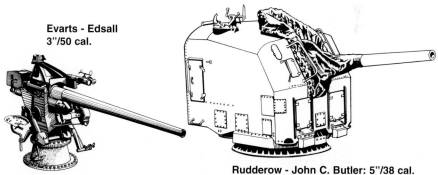

Evarts - Edsall
3"/50 cal.

Rudderow - John C. Butler: 5"/38 cal.

The HODGES (DE-231) shows off her 32-33/3D modified camouflage Measure system on her port side. Compare the design to the starboard side of the HODGES. The HODGES carries the standard main armament of two 5inch/38 caliber mounts. The mooring lines are being readied in preparation for porting. (Floating Drydock)

(Below) The MCNULTY (DE-581) leaves Boston Harbor for sea trials in 1944. She is camouflaged in Measure 22. The black boot topping, delineating the water line, can be seen just below the navy blue paint. (Floating Drydock)

(Above) The RILEY (DE-579) sails out of Boston Harbor on 17 March 1944 for trials in the Atlantic. The RILEY is camouflaged in Measure 22, an effective scheme when there was little chance of aerial attack, such as the mid-Atlantic. Depth charges are fully armed. (Floating Drydock)

(Below) The TINSMAN (DE-589) wearing weathered measure 32/3D paint sails into Boston Harbor in 1944. A HF/DF antenna is fitted to the auxiliary mast and an SA radar mounted atop the main mast. The TINSMAN would go on to serve in the Naval Reserve Training Fleet. (Floating Drydock)

(Above) The METIVIER (DE-582) moving along in calm Atlantic waters in 1944. She is camouflaged in Measure 22. The forward 40mm mount and a pair of 20mm cannons are trained at the photographing aircraft. This combination of anti-aircraft cannons would have been fatal for an attacking aircraft at this range. (Floating Drydock)

(Below) The DANIEL A. JOY (DE-585) shows off her Measure 22 paint scheme during 1944. The main mast is fitted with SA air search radar and the aft mast is fitted with HF/DF high frequency antenna. Following World War Two the DANIEL A. JOY was placed in the Reserve Fleet. (ELSILRAC)

(Above)The LOUGH (DE-586) is being maneuvered to an outfitting pier following her launching from Bethlehem Shipbuilding, Hingham, MA on 22 January 1944. Once she reaches the pier all of the government furnished equipment such as the weapons, masts and electronic items will be installed. The paint scheme is Measure 22. (ELSILRAC)

The BRAY (DE-709) is painted in Measure 31/3D in 1944. An SA air search antenna is atop the main mast, but no surface search radar appears to be fitted. An HF/FD antenna is fitted to the aft mast and a pair of jammer antennas are mounted on the main mast cross bar. (ELSILRAC)

A starboard side view of the HOLT (DE-706) in the Atlantic in 1944. The HOLT was constructed by Defoe at Bay City, Michigan and then sailed down the Mississippi River to the Gulf of Mexico. The main mast is fitted with SA air search and SU sea search antennas. The camouflage scheme is 32-33/3D and appears it may be undergoing a change. (ELSILRAC)

The RUDDEROW (DE-224), the class leader, is painted in the Measure 22 scheme, but without a hull number affixed to the bow — perhaps it was removed by a wartime censor. The RUDDEROW was one of only 22 of the class that was completed as a Destroyer Escort, the other 50 were converted to fast attack transports (APDs). (ELSILRAC)

A starboard bow view of the DE LONG (DE-684) following the Korean Conflict. Armament changes comprised the removal of all 20mm guns and the installation of a quad 40mm mount and a pair of twin 40mm guns on the aft superstructure. The covered item between the bridge and the number one 5incher is the trainable Hedgehog System. (ELSILRAC)

JOHN C. BUTLER CLASS

The JOHN C. BUTLER class was the last class of Destroyer Escorts constructed during World War Two for the U.S. Navy. They were identical in outward appearance to the RUDDEROW class with only an internal change of machinery.

The JOHN C. BUTLER class retained the 306 foot overall hull length as in the earlier classes. Beam and draught remained at 36 feet 10 inches and 11 feet respectively. Displacement rose to 1,275 tons standard and 2,100 tons full war load.

The JOHN C. BUTLER class were fitted with Combustion Engineering 12,000 horsepower boilers that provided steam to Westinghouse geared turbines. The change from General Electric to Westinghouse geared turbines gave the JOHN C. BUTLER the designator of "WGT." The twin screws gave the class a speed of close to 30 knots.

Armament remained the same as the RUDDEROW class with 2 5inch/38 caliber dual purpose enclosed mounts, 2 twin 40mm Bofors anti-aircraft cannons and 12 20mm close in anti-aircraft cannons. A 21 inch triple torpedo launcher was placed on the superstructure. As in the RUDDEROW class, the launcher was eventually replaced by four 40mm single mount cannons.

A total of 85 of the JOHN C. BUTLER class were constructed by Federal, Boston Navy Yard, Consolidated and Brown shipyard, but not all were commissioned during World War Two. The construction of the WAGNER (DE-539) and VANDIVER (DE-540) was halted and the hulls put in storage until 1955. The two hulls were brought out of long term storage and their conversion to Destroyer Escort, Radar (DER) commenced. Once the conversion was completed they joined the other DERs in the "wet" DEW line. They were the only two DERs with steam power.

Four of the JOHN C. BUTLER class were lost during World War Two, with the first three being lost during the month of October 1944. On the 3rd of October the SHELTON (DE-407) was escorting a pair of escort carriers when she was struck by a torpedo fired from the Japanese submarine RO-41. The damage was fatal and she sank just off of the Admiralty Islands. Three weeks later during the battle off Samar, Leyte Gulf, the SAMUEL B. ROBERTS (DE-413) was sunk by Japanese naval gunfire while escorting escort carriers. The Gambier Bay (CVE-73), HOEL (DD-533) and JOHNSTON (DD-557) were also lost during that fateful battle. Three days later during the continuing Leyte Gulf Naval Battle the I-45 sank the EVERSOLE (DE-404) with a torpedo. On 9 May 1945 the OBERRENDER (DE-344) was struck by a Japanese Kamikaze while she was off of Okinawa. She was towed to Kerama Retto for repairs, but the damage was beyond repair and she was expended as a target on 6 November 1945.

The JOHN C. BUTLER (DE-339), class leader, leaving Boston Harbor on 29 May 1944 following a refit. The camouflage scheme is Measure 32/11D. The JOHN C. BUTLER class were steam powered with geared turbine twin screw drives. They were armed with two 5inch dual purpose enclosed mounts. A total of 85 of the JOHN C. BUTLER class were constructed. (Floating Drydock)

The OBERRENDER (DE-344) moving out of Boston Harbor on 15 February 1944. The OBERRENDER was camouflaged in open measure 31-32/22D modified. The OBERRENDER was damaged by a Kamikaze suicide plane off of Okinawa on 9 May 1945. The damage was so severe that repairs were not made; she was sunk as a target following hostilities in the Pacific. (Floating Drydock)

K Gun and Hedgehogs

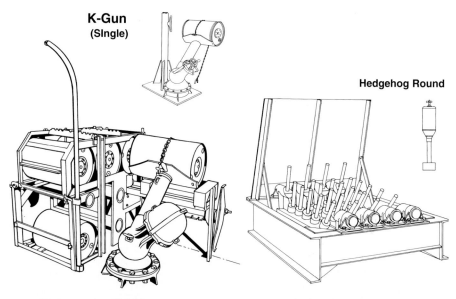

K-Gun
(SIngle)

Hedgehog Round

K-Gun with Roller Loader

Hedgehog Launcher

The RICHARD S. BULL (DE-402) in the Pacific during 1944. She carries Measure 31/3C, a scheme originally drawn for a cruiser, but adapted to a DE. SA and SL radar arrays are fitted to the main mast. The RICHARD S. BULL joined the Pacific Reserve Fleet following World War Two and was expended as a target in 1969. (Floating Drydock)

The ROBERT BRAZIER (DE-345) moving out of the New York Navy Yard on 18 November 1944 to join a convoy bound for Europe. The camouflage scheme is 31/3D, a scheme employed for the North Atlantic in 1944-45. The auxiliary aft mast contains the HF/DF high frequency antenna used to locate surfaced U-boats. (Floating Drydock)

(Below) The STRAUS (DE-408) sailing out to sea following commissioning ceremonies in June 1944. The STRAUS is camouflaged in Measure 31-32/22D an open scheme. The mast contains the SA and SL radar antennas, because of its shape the SA radar antenna was called the "bedspring" antenna. (Floating Drydock)

(Above) The EVERSOLE (DE-404) moving into the Atlantic out of Boston on 20 May 1944. Finished in camouflage scheme 31/3C, she sailed for the Pacific and was sunk on 28 October 1944 in the Battle for Leyte Gulf by the Japanese Submarine I-45. Compare this camouflage scheme with that on the RICHARD S. BULL on page 39. (Floating Drydock)

(Below) The JACCARD (DE-355) was camouflaged in an experimental scheme 32-33/3D and was used to compare various camouflage schemes against Admiralty designs. Measure 32/3D was carried to starboard and 33/3D to port. (Floating Drydock)

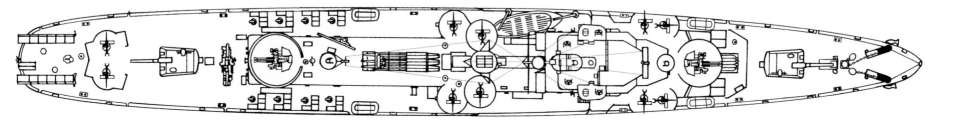

DE 355 USS JACCARD

Length: 306'
Beam: 36'10"
Draft: 11'
Displacement
  Standard: 1275 tons
  Full Load: 2100 tons
Propulsion: 12,000 HP Twin Screws
Speed: 30 Knots
Complement: 215

Armament: 2 x 5"/38 Guns
                     2 x Twin 40mm AA
                     10 x 20mm AA
                     1 x Triple 21" Torpedo Mount
                     1 x Hedgehog System
                     Depth Charges

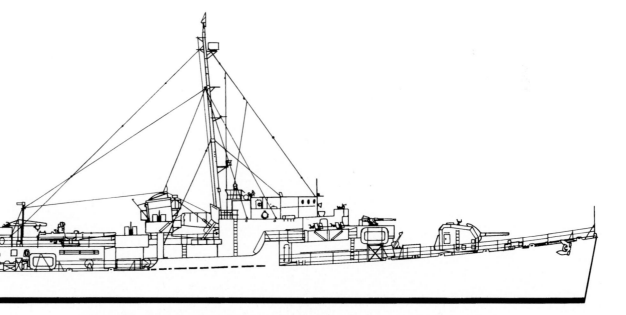

(Above) The GRADY (DE-445) sails past the Statue of Liberty in New York Harbor in 1944. The GRADY is camouflaged in modified Measure 31-32/22D. The GRADY joined the Pacific Reserve Fleet following World War Two, and was stricken in 1968. (Floating Drydock)

(Below) The HOWARD F. CLARK (DE-533) pulls alongside a fleet replenishment ship "somewhere" in the Pacific during 1944. The HOWARD F. CLARK was part of an escort for the Escort Carrier (CVE) in the background. Measure 31/2C paint scheme is carried. The HOWARD F. CLARK was one of the few DEs to be equipped with a quad 40mm mount that replaced the torpedo tubes. (Floating Drydock)

(Above) The FORMOE (DE-509) moving at flank speed in October 1944. The FORMOE was camouflaged in Measure 31/3D. SA and SU radar antennas are fitted to the main mast and the HF/DF antenna is on the mast aft the the torpedo tubes. The FORMOE was given to Portugal following World War Two. (Floating Drydock)

(Above) The KENNETH M. WILLETT (DE-354) sailing into Boston Harbor in September 1944. The camouflage scheme appears to be Measure 21; one month later the ship would be painted in an Admiralty scheme for tests. (Floating Drydock)

(Below) The RAYMOND (DE-341), seen in the Atlantic in 1953, was part of the Pacific Reserve Fleet. The MK-52 radar gun director is in place of the optical range finder on the roof of the wheel house. Following her service in the Reserve Fleet the RAYMOND was stricken in 1972. (Floating Drydock)

(Above) The KENNETH M. WILLETT (DE-354) in 1956 tied up at Bayboro Harbor, St. Petersburg, Florida. All of the 20mm mounts as well as the torpedo tubes have been removed. The ship served in the Reserve Fleet until 1972 when she was stricken from the rolls. (Author)

APD CONVERSIONS

The first Fast Attack Transports (APD) were converted from World War One flush deck destroyers (DD). The MANLEY (DD-74) served as the prototype for the Fast Attack Transport, with conversions beginning in 1938. Thirty-six of the flush deck destroyers were converted, which consisted of removing two of the boilers to increase storage, all torpedo tubes and either one or two of the stacks, depending on the class. The removal of the two boilers severely affected the speed, but increased cargo capacity. Further conversions included the installation of four boat davits to handle four LCVP landing craft. Conversion from DD to APD of the old flush deckers was not as successful as the later conversion of Destroyer Escorts to Fast Attack Transports.

Conversion of Destroyer Escorts to Fast Attack Transports was authorized in 1944 by Admiral Ernest King. The CHARLES LAWRENCE (DE-53), a BUCKLEY class "TE" was the first of the DEs converted to the APD configuration and was numbered APD-37, becoming the class leader. The CROSLEY (DE-226) was the first of the "TEVs" to be converted and was designated APD-87. The conversion of a DE to an APD included removal of the torpedo tubes and the aft 1.1 quad or 40mm anti-aircraft cannon and the number 3 3inch gun. A cargo crane was placed in the position formerly occupied by the aft weapons. A pair of 40mm cannons were placed on each side of the crane. There were two different designs of cargo cranes employed, either a vertical pillar crane or a tripod crane, both of which were steam powered. The number one and two 3inch guns were replaced by a single enclosed 5inch/38 dual purpose cannon. An enlarged superstructure, with a high freeboard, was built amidship for housing troops. Over the superstructure was constructed two boat davits and cradles to handle LCVPs. The sonar and two depth charge tracks were retained to combat submarine threats.

Two types of Destroyer Escorts were involved in the conversion to APD. The BUCKLEY "TE" and RUDDEROW "TEV" class were selected for conversion, both of which were steam powered and long hulled (306 feet overall in length). Displacement for the APDs rose to 1,725 tons standard and 2,114 full war load. Rated speed was 24 knots, and with onboard fuel of 347 tons range was 12,000 nautical miles at an economical speed of 12 knots. Armament consisted of a 5inch/38 caliber dual purpose cannon plus six 40mm Bofors cannons in twin mounts and six 20mm cannons in single mounts.

The APDs were used to carry a heavily armed battalion of Marines or Army Rangers to secure beachheads on Japanese held Pacific Islands. During a mission the deck of an AP would be covered with supplies and vehicles to be used during an invasion. Once the invasion point was reached, the LCVPs would be off loaded and the troops and equipment would be taken ashore by the landing craft. The APDs were also used by the Underwater Demolition Teams (UDT), "Frogmen."

The LLOYD (APD-63 ex DE-209) was chosen to be the flagship of a fast attack transport division. The LANING (APD-55 ex DE-159) and the HOLLIS (APD-86 ex DE-794) were used as UDT Flagships. No crane was fitted to the LANING, instead a twin 40mm Bofors cannon was installed in its place. The FECHTELER (DE-157) was slated to be converted to the APD-53, but she was sunk in the Mediterranean by a U-boat torpedo in 1944. The BATES (APD-47 ex DE-68) was sunk off of Okinawa when she was hit by a Kamikaze on 25 May 1945.

A total of 95 APDs were converted and they performed valuable service during World War Two, landing troops on by-passed islands during the island hopping campaign of the Pacific Theater as well as inserting UDT teams to clear beach obstacles.

Following World War Two many of the APDs were given to U.S. Allies serving well into the 1990's.

The CROSLEY (APD-87) was the former DE-226, a RUDDEROW class Destroyer Escort converted to a Fast Attack Transport for use in the Pacific. The conversion to APD included the addition of a derrick crane on the quarter-deck to load supplies onto the four Landing Craft (LCVP) and the fitting of a deckhouse amidship. (ELSILRAC)

The LLOYD (APD-63 ex DE-209), was a BUCKLEY class DE before her conversion to a Fast Attack Transport. THE LLOYD was the Flagship for the Pacific APD Division. The fore and aft decks are covered with supplies that will be used in a Pacific Island invasion. The LLOYD was converted by Philadelphia Navy Yard in 1944. Note the difference in the cranes between the LLOYD and the CROSLEY. (Floating Drydock)

The jungle pattern camouflage shows up quite well on the BATES (APD-47). The BATES was the former DE-68, a BUCKLEY Class DE. The BATES was sunk off of Okinawa on the night of 23 May 1945 by a Japanese Kamikaze suicide plane. The BATES had a vertical pillar type of cargo crane on the deck. A 5inch/38 enclosed mount and twin 40mm Bofors cannons replaced the 3inch open mounts. (Floating Drydock)

The HORACE A. BASS (APD-124) was the ex DE-691, a RUDDEROW class Destroyer Escort converted to a high speed transport in 1945. The HORACE A. BASS appears to be camouflaged in Measure 21, solid navy blue, a scheme deemed to be most effective against aerial attacks, especially Kamikazes. SA and SU radar are fitted to the main mast. The signal flags spell out N-U-C-X. (Floating Drydock)

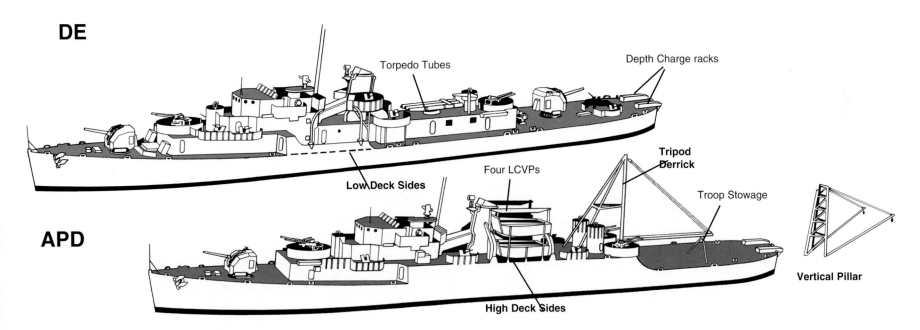

DE

Torpedo Tubes

Depth Charge racks

Tripod Derrick

Troop Stowage

Low Deck Sides

Four LCVPs

APD

High Deck Sides

Vertical Pillar

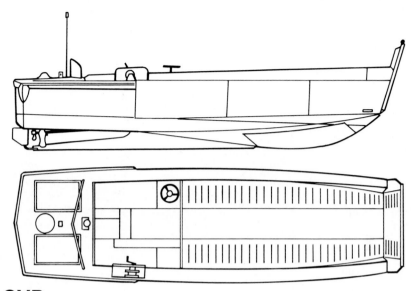

LCVP

(Above) The boat davits and cradles for the four LCVP landing craft on the HORACE A. BASS (APD-124) as she undergoes a refitting. The four LCVPs would be used to land a light battalion of Army or Marines from the APD. The crane was used to load supplies from the APD to the LCVP once the landings commenced. (Floating Drydock)

(Below) The REDNOUR (APD-102) was the ex DE-592, a RUDDEROW class DE. She is camouflaged in Measure 31/20L a scheme that was effective for jungle concealment. The REDNOUR was sold to the Mexican Navy in 1969 and renamed the COAHUILA (B.07). The SU radar was placed low on the mast on an extension. (Floating Drydock)

(Above) The crew of the REGISTER (APD-92) ex DE-233 is assembled on the foc'sle as the ship undergoes a change of command in 1945. The REGISTER carries a splotched pattern camouflage design. ADPs were used to land Underwater Demolition Teams (UDTs), raiding teams, and invasion troops during the island hopping campaigns in the Pacific. (ELSILRAC)

(Below) The LANING (APD-55 ex DE-159) was outfitted as the UDT Flagship in the Pacific. The deck crane was replaced by twin 40mm cannons. The LANING, as a Flagship, carried increased radio gear. Only two LCVPs are installed on the boat davits. (Floating Drydock)

(Above) The LIDDLE (APD-60 ex DE-206) was a converted BUCKLEY Class DE, at pier side, Bayboro Harbor, St. Petersburg, Florida in 1956. The LIDDLE served as a training ship for the Atlantic reserve Forces. No LCVPs are fitted to the boat davits. The LIDDLE was a highly decorated veteran of World War Two. (Author)

DER CONVERSIONS

When the Japanese began using suicide planes (Kamikazes) against the Allied fleets in the Pacific as early as 1943, a method to provide early warning was sought.

The solution was to place US. and Allied Destroyers (DDs) and Destroyer Escorts (DEs) on what became known as a picket line. The picket line was placed between the Allied fleet and the Japanese. By using their air search radar, the picket line provided early warning for the fleet, but it came at a high price for the Destroyers and Destroyer Escorts. During the April-May 1945 campaign for Okinawa 22 US Destroyers hit by Kamikaze aircraft were either sunk or so severely damaged that they never returned to service. The last U.S. Navy ship sunk by a Kamikaze was the CALLAGHAN (DD-792) on 28 July 1945. Nine days later the US. dropped an atomic bomb on Hiroshima leading to the end of the Pacific conflict.

During the Korean war there was again a need for early warning protection, not only for the U.S. Fleet in the Pacific, but the continental United States. Under Ship Characteristics Board Program 468 (SCB-468) thirty-four EDSALL "FMR" class and two JOHN C. BUTLER "WGT" Destroyer Escorts were converted to Destroyer Escort, Radar (DER). The "FMR" were diesel powered and the "WGT" were steam powered. The two steam powered DERs were the WAGNER (DER-539) and VANDIVIER (DER-540). Construction of the two ships commenced in 1943 at the Boston Navy Yard. Construction was halted at wars end and the ships were placed in long term storage in an uncompleted state. In 1954 they were removed from storage and conversion to DER status began.

The conversion from DE to DER was extensive and included an enlargement and rebuild of the mid ship main deck superstructure with aluminum to house the increased electronic gear. The modified superstructure resembled the DE converted Fast Attack Transport (APD) in configuration. The Combat Information Center (CIC) was moved down two decks below the bridge and the mess area was moved to the starboard midship. The single pole main mast was replaced with an aluminum tripod mast that contained electronic countermeasure (ECM) and Tactical Air Navigation (TACAN) antennas. Aft of the enlarged deckhouse was placed another tripod mast for the SPS-8 height finder radar. SPS-10 air-search and SPS-28 sea-search were fitted to the main mast.

The weapons suite was upgraded with radar controlled 3inch/50 caliber dual purpose cannons in open and enclosed mounts, however, the WAGNER and VANDIVER retained their original 5inch/38 caliber weapons. For anti-submarine warfare (ASW) duties a single roller track was retained on the starboard stern area and a MK-15 trainable Hedgehog system was situated in the place of the former number two 3inch gun mount. During rebuilds six triple MK-44 12.75inch ASW torpedo tube launchers were installed.

DERs were used in mid-ocean under the sea frontier and fleet commands in the "wet" Distant Early Warning (DEW) line covering segments of the Continental Air Defense (CONAD) system. Reports of unidentified aircraft were reported to CONAD. DERs served in this capacity until 1965 when the "DEW" line was dissestablished.

Twelve of the DERs reverted back to Destroyer Escort status with the removal of the TACAN and SPS-8 radar. Converted DE's were sent to Vietnam and operated in the South China Sea and off Taiwan during operation "Market Time." When South Vietnam fell to the forces of the North in 1975 the FORSTER (DER-344) which had been transferred to South Vietnam was captured. She was renamed TRAN KHANH DU and served as a training ship well into the 1990's with the naval forces of Viet Nam.

The CAMP (DER-251) was the ex DE-251 converted to a Radar Picket Ship in 1956. The conversion included the installation of two tripod masts with increased radar and increased upper deck spaces for radio and radar equipment operators. The CAMP was a former EDSALL class DE. Trainable Hedgehogs (MK-15s) were placed in the former 3inch gun position. During World War Two the CAMP had been converted with 5/38s replacing the 3inch mounts. (ELSILRAC)

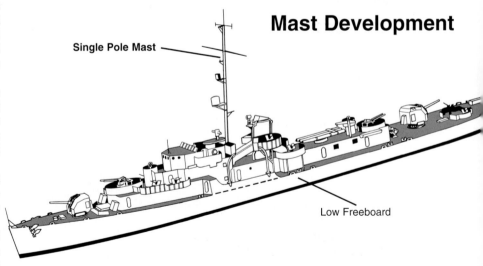

Mast Development

Single Pole Mast

Low Freeboard

Destroyer Escort (DE)

(Above) The KRETCHMER (DER-329) in 1958. She was assigned to the Atlantic Distant Early Warning Airborne Wing. DERs a threat to both enemy aircraft and submarines. DER's retained their Hedgehogs, depth charge roller racks and in addition most were fitted with ASW torpedoes. The KRETCHMER is painted in Measure 27, with the deck painted navy blue. (ELSILRAC)

(Below Right) The Brister (DER 327) was one of 36 DERs to serve in the Atlantic and Pacific under the Sea Frontier and Fleet Commands. The Brister served in the Pacific out of Guam, reporting uniditified aircraft and ships directly to Continental Air Defense (CONAD). (ELSILRAC)

(Above) The WAGNER (DER-539) was converted to DER status in 1955 and joined the Atlantic DEW" force. The WAGNER and her sister ship VANDIVIER (DER-540) were both launched in 1943, but stored uncompleted. In 1955 construction and conversion was undertaken to DER configuration. The WAGNER and VANDIVIER were the only two DERs to be steam powered having been converted from the JOHN C. BUTLER class. (ELSILRAC)

Mast Development

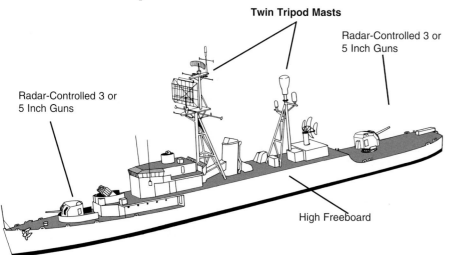

Twin Tripod Masts

Radar-Controlled 3 or 5 Inch Guns

Radar-Controlled 3 or 5 Inch Guns

High Freeboard

Destroyer Escort Radar (DER)

4001 U-Boats in action

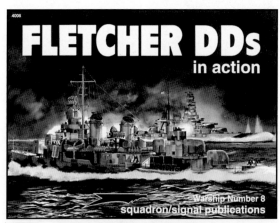

4008 Fletcher DDs in action

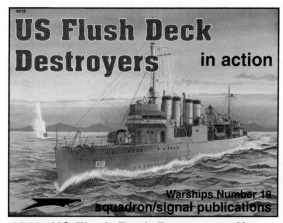

4019 US Flush Deck Destroyers i/a

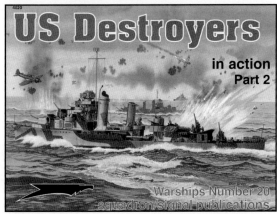

4020 US Destroyers in action Part 2

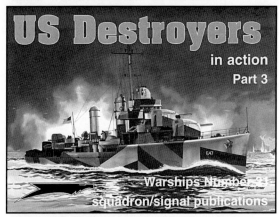

4021 US Destroyers in action Part 3

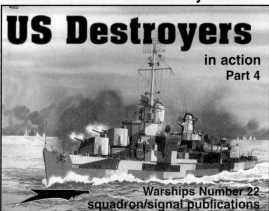

4022 US Destroyers in action Part 4

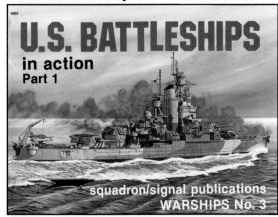

4003 US Battleships in action Part 1

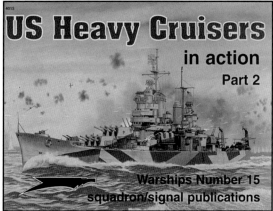

4015 US Heavy Cruisers in action Part 2

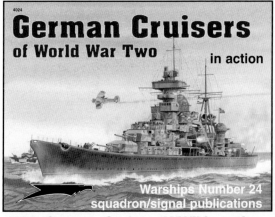

4024 German Cruisers WWII in action